# Daniel Harrington Fairbanks the Third and a Day on the Farm

Todd Zoellick

Illustrated by: Joshua Allen

AuthorHouse™
1663 Liberty Drive
Bloomington, IN 47403
www.authorhouse.com
Phone: 1-800-839-8640

Published by AuthorHouse  10/23/2012

ISBN:       978-1-4772-8408-7 (sc)

Library of Congress Control Number: 2012920005

To my readers:  Always celebrate your own uniqueness, and recognize that differences in others, either real or perceived, are those wonderful details that make our world a far more interesting place.

"Each second we live in a new and unique moment of the universe, a moment that never was before and will never be again.  And what do we teach our children in school?  We teach them that two and two makes four, and that Paris is the capital of France.  When will we also teach them what they are?  We should say to each of them:  Do you know what you are?  You are a marvel.  You are unique.  In all of the world there is no other child exactly like you.  In the millions of years that have passed there has never been another child like you.  And look at your body—what a wonder it is!  Your legs, your arms, your cunning fingers, the way you move!  You may become a Shakespeare, a Michelangelo, a Beethoven.  You have the capacity for anything.  Yes, you are a marvel."

--Pablo Casals

There's a great little town not too far from us here
Where a boy and his dog live with friends who are near.
The dog's name is Clark, and the boy's name you have heard.
He is called Daniel Harrington Fairbanks the Third.

Both the boy and his dog are together each day,
And they often invite other friends to come play.
But there's one special friend Clark and Daniel adore.
Their best friend's name is Brooke, and she lives right next door.

On a crisp, autumn day, Daniel's parents pack up
The car for a trip with Daniel, Brooke, and the pup.
They will visit some friends on a farm far away
That the children and dog can explore for the day.

After driving awhile, they can finally see
The farmhouse, barn, and fields just as plain as can be.
They jump out of the car and begin to explore.
There's so much they can do that they've not done before.

There are fields all around growing food they can eat.
They taste corn on the cob, and it's ever so sweet.
Even Clark has a taste, and it's really quite good.
They'd eat corn from the field everyday if they could.

While the three eat their corn, something wanders close by.
It's the farmer's grey cat, and it catches Clark's eye.
The cat's name is Meow—the same noise that she makes.
With Clark's growling and barking, the scared Meow shakes.

Even though up to now, Clark has not met a cat.
The grey cat's unlike Clark, and he doesn't like that.
Clark runs after the cat at a very fast pace,
With both Daniel and Brooke quickly joining the chase.

Meow lives on the farm and knows just where to go.
She hides inside the barn in a place they don't know.
The friends get to the barn, and there's so much to see.
But Clark thinks to himself, *These things don't look like me.*

The first thing in the barn that they see is a cow
Being milked by a man who has started just now.
Clark has never seen something like this in the past.
It seems strange, and he barks while he runs away fast.

As he runs from the cow, right in front of his nose
He sees sheep being sheared to make people new clothes.
Clark has never seen something like this in the past.
It seems strange, and he barks while he runs away fast.

Once he's out of the barn, Clark sees chickens outside.
They're all laying new eggs as he watches wide-eyed.
Clark has never seen something like this in the past.
It seems strange, and he barks while he runs away fast.

The next thing that he sees is a man on a horse.
It has four legs like him but much bigger, of course.
Clark has never seen something like this in the past.
It seems strange, and he barks while he runs away fast.

While the friends ran around and explored the whole place,
The cat followed behind, leaving plenty of space.
Being out of the barn, Clark can now clearly see
That the cat is nearby, closer than she should be.

Clark runs after the cat, barking loudly to say,
*I will get you this time; you will not get away!*
The cat runs through a stream to avoid getting caught,
But the water is much deeper than she had thought.

Meow falls in the stream, and this cat cannot swim.
Clark knows saving the cat is now all up to him.
He jumps right in the stream, and he pulls the cat out.
Clark would do the right thing; there was never a doubt.

After saving Meow, Clark discovers at last
That cats aren't all that bad as he'd thought in the past.
Meow thanks Clark for helping by licking his nose.
They both find they're alike as their new friendship grows.

Clark has learned something new in the farmyard today.
Every creature has skills, and they're all on display.
All the chickens lay eggs, and the sheep give their wool.
The horses give rides, and cows are milked when they're full.

Clark has seen many things he had not seen before,
And though they're unlike him, he's not scared anymore.
All have something to offer, as Clark can now see,
And he aims to become the best dog he can be.

CPSIA information can be obtained
at www.ICGtesting.com
Printed in the USA
LVIW012043301012

305146LV00001B

9 781477 284087